W9-BAJ-108

Jeremy's Tail

by Duncan Ball

illustrated by
Donna Rawlins

Orchard Books ~ New York

This is the story of Jeremy, who was
determined
to pin the tail on the donkey.

He put on a blindfold, turned around three
times, and walked toward the donkey.

j42706

After a minute someone asked,
"Where are you going?"

"I'm going to pin the tail on the donkey,"
said Jeremy. "How am I doing?"

"You're doing fine," the same voice said.

"Good. Then I'll just keep going straight
ahead."

Children were crowding all around him.
Jeremy could hear them whispering.

"Am I nearly there?" he asked.
"Almost," a boy said. "But watch your step."

Jeremy thought he might be going in the
wrong direction, but then he heard someone
shout, "Straight ahead!"

"Thank you," said Jeremy. "But please don't
give me any hints."

It seemed to Jeremy that the floor
was tipping. I must be getting dizzy, he thought.
What fun!

"What's that tail for?" asked a little voice.

"I'm going to pin the tail on the donkey,"
 said Jeremy.

"I see," the little voice said. "Then you'd better
 keep on walking."

Someone said something that Jeremy didn't understand.

"Don't tell me where the donkey is," Jeremy warned him.

And the same voice said, "Yes, yes. Donkey, donkey."

"Am I getting warmer?" Jeremy asked.

"Yes, yes. Warmer, warmer," a boy said, and Jeremy heard giggles.

Jeremy tripped, and his foot splashed
right into something wet.

"Watch where you put
your lemonade," said Jeremy.
But everyone kept on chattering.

Once more Jeremy called out,
"Hey, how am I doing?"

And a boy with a deep voice said,
"Why don't you take off the
blindfold and see for yourself?"

"That would be cheating,"
Jeremy said.

Then someone must have opened a window
because Jeremy could feel a breeze
blowing against his face.

"It's all right if you whisper," Jeremy said to his
friends. "Just don't tell me where the
donkey is. That would be cheating."

Nobody did, and Jeremy walked on.

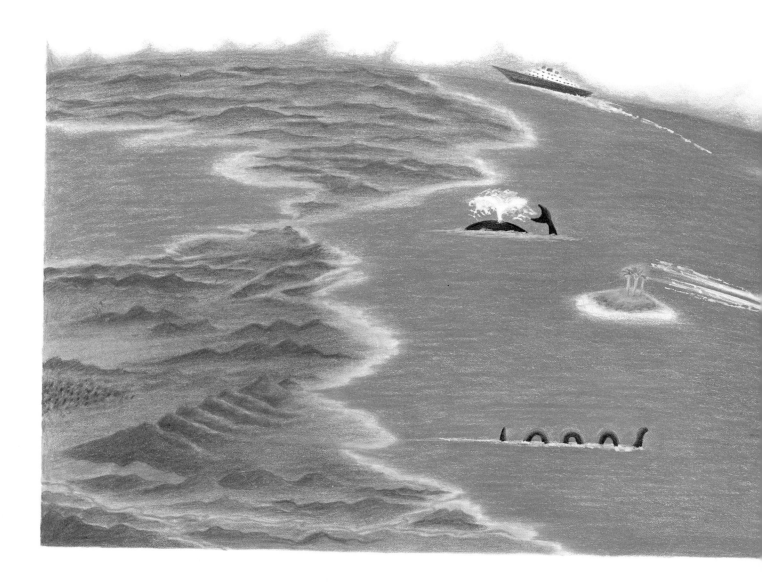

"Where are you going?" a girl asked.

"To the donkey," said Jeremy. "I'm going to pin this tail on him—right smack on his bottom where it belongs."

"I see," said the girl. "Watch your step."

"Here comes the Mighty Masked Marvel!"
  one of the boys yelled.

"Hey," cried Jeremy. "Let me go!
  It's only me."

"We'll let you go, all right," another boy said.

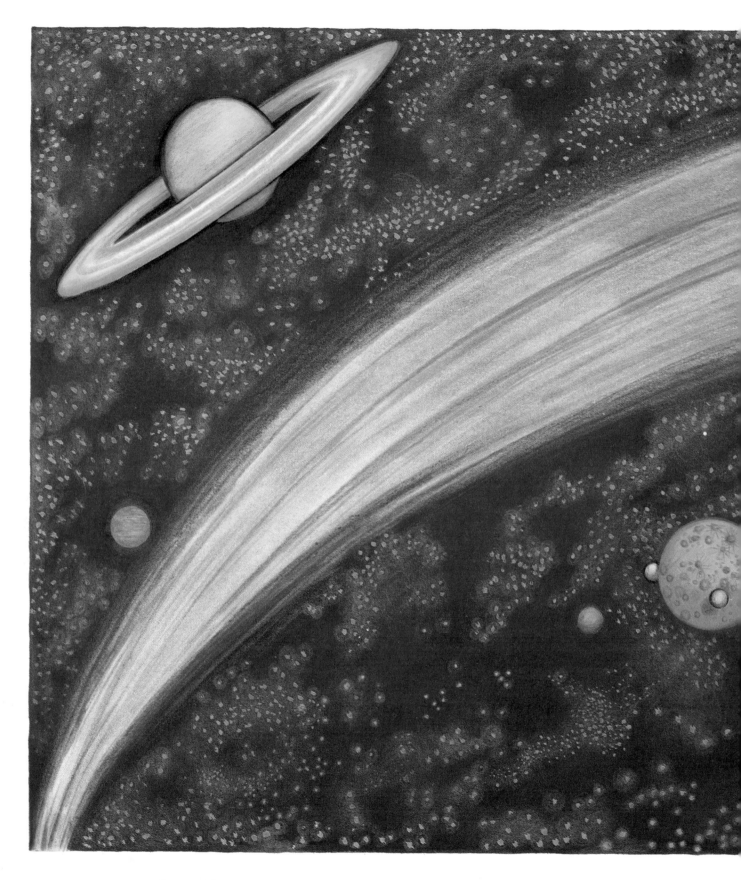

Then there was a loud BOOM!

"Hey, don't trip me," Jeremy protested. "That's not fair."

"Have you pinned the tail on the donkey yet?" someone asked.

"No," said Jeremy. "But I must be getting very close by now."

And on Jeremy went.

And on.

And on.

And at last
Jeremy pinned the tail
on the donkey.

"You peeked," a girl said.

"No, I didn't," said Jeremy.

"You must have, Jeremy. I'm sorry,
  but you'll have to do it again."

Once more
Jeremy put on his blindfold, turned
around three times, and walked
toward the donkey.

So this is the story of Jeremy, who was
determined
to pin the tail on the donkey. . . .

For Saiping   —D.B.
For Julie   —D.R.

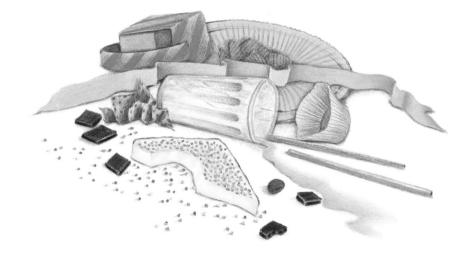

Text copyright © 1990 by Duncan Ball
Illustrations copyright © 1990 by Donna Rawlins
First American Edition 1991 published by Orchard Books
First published in 1990 by Ashton Scholastic Pty Limited (Inc. in NSW)

ORCHARD BOOKS   A division of Franklin Watts, Inc.
387 Park Avenue South   New York, NY 10016

Manufactured in the United States of America
Printed by General Offset Company, Inc.   Bound by Horowitz/Rae
Book design by Alice Lee Groton

10 9 8 7 6 5 4 3 2 1

The text of this book is set in 18 point ITC Zapf International Light.
The illustrations are colored pencil.

Library of Congress Cataloging-in-Publication Data
Ball, Duncan, date.
   Jeremy's tail / by Duncan Ball ; illustrated by Donna Rawlins. —
1st American ed.   p.   cm.
"First published in 1990 by Ashton Scholastic . . . in NSW"—T.p. verso.
Summary: Blindfolded Jeremy, on his way to pin the tail on the
donkey, takes a circuitous route that carries him far afield, over
the ocean and into space, before he finally reaches his goal.
ISBN 0-531-05951-0. — ISBN 0-531-08551-1 (lib. bdg.)
[1. Voyages and travels—Fiction.]   I. Rawlins, Donna, ill.
II. Title.   PZ7.B1985Je 1991   [E]—dc20   90-28952